OLD BLUE
TILLEY

OLD BLUE TILLEY

Robbie Branscum

MACMILLAN PUBLISHING COMPANY
New York

COLLIER MACMILLAN CANADA
Toronto

MAXWELL MACMILLAN INTERNATIONAL PUBLISHING GROUP
New York · *Oxford* · *Singapore* · *Sydney*

Macmillan Publishing Company
866 Third Avenue
New York, NY 10022
Collier Macmillan Canada, Inc.
1200 Eglinton Avenue East
Suite 200
Don Mills, Ontario M3C 3N1
First edition
Printed in the United States of America

10 9 8 7 6 5 4 3 2 1

The text of this book is set in 12 point Cheltenham Book
Designed by REM Studio, Inc.

Library of Congress Cataloging-in-Publication Data
Branscum, Robbie.
Old Blue Tilley/
by Robbie Branscum.—1st ed.
p.   cm.
Summary: Orphaned, fourteen-year-old Hambone accompanies the
circuit-riding preacher, Old Blue Tilley, on his rounds high up in
Ozark mountains and everywhere they go they find that Oxalee,
Old Blue's sworn enemy, has been there before them.
ISBN 0-02-711931-9
[1. Ozark Mountains—Fiction. 2. Mountain life—Fiction.]
I. Title.
PZ7.B7375401 1991
[Fic]—dc20   90-6348   CIP

To John Kelley—
and to all the other preachers
I know,
and to Mark Moore
for being there

One

"Hey hi, hey hi ho,
Old Blue Tilley's a-gonna save some souls.
Preach 'bout hell, preach 'bout fire.
Preach 'bout women who bob thar hair."

The song came drifting down the mountain-side on a blue haze, sending the blood leaping through my veins. Old Blue was back and he would come to get me. I ran out by the spring waiting for more, holding my breath. Then it came, cheerfully dancing over the waterfall and giant bluffs.

1

"Hambone. Hambone, where ye been?
'Round the world and gone ag'in.
Whatcha gonna do when ye git thare?
Sit me right down in my rockin' chair."

Since I was Hambone, I knew what that meant. It was spring and Old Blue was coming to get me to ride his circuit with him. Going deep and high in the mountains and valleys, visiting folks who hadn't seen a new face all year. Then when the visiting was over there would be a big three-day revival where all the folks would meet for the last time until another year rolled around and Old Blue rode the circuit again.

Old Blue had been to town seeing about help for the poor hill families and gathering the news about whether we were going to go to war with Germany or not. I hoped not; it seemed as though I had enough to worry about right here at home.

Old Blue wanted me to be a preacher, too, but danged if I would. I didn't see nothing lovable at all in the people Old Blue loved. In fact, I reckoned Old Blue was about all the human I could stand, and lots of time I didn't like him very much.

I picked up the ax leaning by the cabin door and went to the woodpile to chop kindling for the cast-iron cookstove. It would be awhile before Old Blue got here, and since I was living at his cabin,

I figured it was only right to have him some food ready.

That had been four years ago, when I come to live with him, and he had never asked me to leave or nothing and I didn't feel too bad. I mean, I earned my keep. My folks had died, and since none of the kinfolks had offered to take me in, I just flat started walking. A couple of uncles had taken over the farm that was supposed to be mine. I bet neither of them ever bothered to look for me and I reckoned they hoped I was dead. I sure hoped they were dead, so I wouldn't have to kill them when I finally went home.

Anyhow, I just started walking, I didn't know where, until Old Blue found me half-starved. Old Blue taught me a lot of things, like how to read the Bible, do my sums, and how to cook and hunt. Of course, Old Blue didn't know that in my mind I had my uncles in my gun sight instead of the little squirrels. He also taught me how to take care of the cabin and the animals while he was gone on his circuit ride, or if he was out doctoring folks.

I reckoned to folks living so far apart that a preacher was everything to them, and I sort of thought maybe Old Blue was hoping I'd take his place when he got too old, 'cause he had taught me how to doctor folks—and animals, too.

Old Blue was getting old, reckon he was forty-five if he was a day. His long beard and his hair was becoming gray, but his overall figure was still tall and straight and his eyes spit blue fire when he preached or were soft and blue as a rain-washed April day when he looked at old folks or newborn things.

Now he would be home again soon, riding Brimstone, his mule. He named him Brimstone 'cause he said it took something full of hell to climb the mountainside where he went. Everybody knew Brimstone was mean as hell and twice as stubborn. Nobody but Old Blue could handle him. Me and that mule were the only close family Old Blue had.

Old Blue didn't even know my name 'cause I wouldn't tell him. I was afraid if I did he would find some of my kinfolks and make me live with them and I didn't want to live with uncles who had taken my farm away in the first place. I had gnawed all the meat from a ham bone the first day he brought me home, so that's why he called me "Hambone."

I carried the chopped kindling into the cabin and started a fire in the old stove and the fireplace, too, 'cause the spring days still had a shirttail hold on winter. The cabin was roomier than most. Old Blue had built it himself with the rock fireplace across one wall and the cast-iron cookstove across on the other wall. There were an oak table and chairs and rockers made from river-bottom cane, a bed built in a corner and a ladder going up to the loft where I slept. There were warm deer skins on the split-logged floor and a bear skin before the fireplace that Old Blue was plum proud of. Deer antlers hung above the fireplace and held Old Blue's shotgun when he was home and my twenty-two. It was all I carried away from my old home with me.

Outside the cabin, a small waterfall leaped off the dark rocks of a bluff to a spring dugout beneath it. It was big enough to hold the fish, keeping them fresh, and the water was ice cold to drink. There was a garden spot behind the cabin and a fenced-in barn behind that. It held one hog, Brimstone, and my own mule, Sam. I mean, it was a real comfortable life and I didn't see why Old Blue wanted to leave it to go help folks that seemed to me should be left alone to sin all they wanted. I didn't admit it to myself, but I was plum ready for company, being more than a mile tired of my own.

I felt sort of excited about Old Blue coming home to take me with him. Course, I was more excited about the camping out and hunting food than I was about seeing folks I didn't care about one way or the other.

One reason I didn't care about folks was because they always stared at me. I mean, I always knew I was double ugly, but folks had no right pointing it out. My eyes are a gooseberry green, not a pretty green at all. And my hair, the color of bland carrots; and you couldn't lay a dime on my face unless it covered two dozen freckles; and to top it all off, I'm as skinny as a bean pole, no matter how much I eat.

Thinking of eating, I pushed a pot of beans on the stove to heat and dashed up to the spring for some fresh cold water. By the time Old Blue rode up to the barn, corn bread was browning in the oven. I didn't run to meet him or nothing, but truth to tell, I sort of wanted to. I mean, he had been gone over a month and I hadn't seen a human since he left. But for some reason, I didn't want him to know I was proud he was home; he would think he had a hold on me of some sort.

I didn't trust adults. I mean, they had never done much for me, except dying on me and kinfolks easing out the door before they could be asked to take me home with them. No matter how I felt, I knew dang good and well, I did owe Old Blue for taking me in, so I worked hard keeping his place up good. I mean, I believed in paying my debts, though Old Blue never said I owed him anything.

Suddenly, his bulk was filling the doorway, his eyes taking in the logged walls I had whitewashed while he was gone, and he said, "Boy, I built me a house, but ye made it a home." I was glad he liked it, but said nothing while I put supper on the table.

Old Blue pulled up a chair, bowed his head,

6

and said, "Lord, I thank Ye fer a safe trip home and fer the boy heer, this food and most ever'thin' Ye can think of. I am a blessed man. Help me to al'ays be thankful and mindful of whare all the blessin's come from. Amen."

I had bowed my head, too, but I didn't pray, I never prayed. God didn't answer me when I begged Him to let Pa and Ma live and I didn't see any reason He would hear me now. I didn't think Old Blue knew he nursed a viper to his bosom—as far as religion was concerned—me, I mean.

Old Blue took a piece of corn bread and stared at it like it was going to bite him back, saying, "Boy, I rode through Potter Valley on the way home and folks is a-gonna git a school thare come fall. Ye might just sit yer thinkin' cap on it. They's gonna be a city teacher, too."

"I ain't a-gonna go to school," I said stubbornly. "I can already read."

"Readin' ain't ever'thin'," Old Blue said, and started to eat.

Course, I didn't tell Old Blue, but I really wanted to go to school. I wanted to learn lots of stuff, but schools had girls in them, and girls made me sweat even on the coldest winter day.

Suddenly, without knowing I was going to, I blurted, "How's come ye never wed, Blue?"

Old Blue stopped chewing and his eyes went soft and he said, "I almost did wed once, a long time ago, but reckon I felt God's call to shepherd His people stronger than the call to wed."

"What happened to yer sweetheart?" I asked curiously.

"She wed somebody else," Old Blue said shortly, and started eating again.

"Shepherd God's people," I snorted to myself, I never seen a people less like God's as the folks Old Blue spent his life on. Old Blue said a body wasn't supposed to judge, but I couldn't seem to help it. I mean, like Oxalee: Everybody knew he was the blackest sinner around and not 'cause his hair, beard, and eyes were coal black, but because his heart was, so folks said.

Oxalee was the thorn in Old Blue's side, and instead of hating Oxalee like I would, Old Blue prayed for him. Somebody said once that Old Blue and Oxalee had been the best of friends long ago, but nobody seemed to know what had happened between them. Only Oxalee and Old Blue knew that, but neither would talk about it.

Old Blue pushed back from the table, saying, "Wal, boy, ye best git ready. We leave 'fore daybreak."

My heart beat faster; I would be with people again, even if I didn't like them. Me and Old Blue Tilley was gonna ride.

Two

It was nippy cold when we woke, the sky was just a faint rose in the east. Old Blue made his circuit ride through the mountains once a year come spring, and for the last four years I went with him. We rode the mules, Brimstone and Sam, without saddles, just blankets between the mules and our rear ends. Behind us were tied our bedrolls, guns, salt, coffee, and an old pot blackened by years of camp fires.

Dipping my face in the spring had taken all the

sleeplessness out of me, and Old Blue dipped his head, snorting like a horse, and we were on our way, full of ham and leftover corn bread.

The first night we would camp, but the next day we would start hitting the homes of Old Blue's flock. I thought Old Blue looked funny, his beard came to the bib of his overalls and his feet nigh touched the ground on each side of the mule.

It seemed we climbed straight up as the sun rose. I took deep breaths of the cedar and pine air, feeling alive from the roots of my hair to the tips of my toes. I sort of wished we had a car or a pickup, but Old Blue said that mules were the only things that could climb our mountains.

Fact of the matter, maybe everyone would have to ride mules if the war with Germany came like folks said it would. Our battery radio said so, too, or was it Old Blue? I mean, that war was coming. I was glad Old Blue was too old to go to war. Well, there's no war just yet, so a body can relax and enjoy himself, I thought, nudging Sam to catch up with Brimstone.

The sun beat down warm on my back, but there were still snowdrifts under the darkness of the trees and the drifts got deeper the higher we climbed. Waterfalls tumbled down the mountainsides, filling the air with music of their own. In sunny open places, birds built nests and young gray and red squirrels played up and down the tree trunks. At noon we stopped by a spring to drink the cold, clear water and

10

to let the mules drink and feed awhile on some new grass.

As ever, Pa and Ma came to my mind when I was in the woods. Our farm had been in the woods near a stream, too, and I could remember how Ma and Pa walked the stream. They would watch me catch the red crawdads and black tadpoles to play with and laugh. I could always hear their happy laughter singing over the top of the pine trees.

I walked around in the woods, resting my back from the hard climb, and shot two young squirrels for our supper, cleaning and skinning them at the spring. Old Blue sat in the sun and read his Bible. I didn't see why he did that; I mean, it seemed to me he knew the Bible by heart anyway. We sat in silence for a little while, then drank again before we climbed on the mules. I was beginning to be hungry again, but knew we wouldn't stop to eat until we made camp for the night.

As we climbed, the snow grew deeper under the cedars and pines, the air so clear and cold it bit your lungs. Vapor blew from the mules' noses like little white clouds, and mine and Old Blue's breath hung in puffs around our faces. My blood was so alive in my veins it seemed to dance.

Sometimes we saw grouse or deer, and once in a while a turkey. My fingers itched for my gun, but Old Blue would never let me kill something unless we needed it to eat and sometimes not even then. Truth to tell, most of the time I didn't like to kill nothing, either, except squirrels or rabbits, there were so many of them. But of course, I liked to eat better than most anything, and if I had been hungry enough the way I was when Old Blue found me, I would have tried to kill and eat a grizzly bear with a teaspoon.

The sun was setting when we reached the stream of water where we always camped the first night out. I gathered wood and built a fire while Old Blue fed the mules some grain from his pack. I spitted the squirrels on green sticks, rubbing them with salt to broil, and Old Blue had the coffee boiling before long. This was one of the times I liked best, sitting and toasting myself at the fire with the smell of roasting meat and coffee in my nose and the singing of pine in my ears.

"Ye think Oxalee will be at the revival ag'in this year, Blue?" I half yawned.

"Wal, he ain't missed one yet," Old Blue said dryly.

"Reckon he will have his old pickup full of whiskey?" I said, half admiring. I mean, Oxalee was a black sinner, but I guess I was a sinner, too, 'cause I never went to the mourners' bench at revival time. Course, I wouldn't have the nerve to sell whiskey at Old Blue's revival the way Oxalee did. But I knew it took a brave man to face Old Blue's fire-and-brimstone meetings and Oxalee sat through every meeting, never turning a hair; like a rock he was.

12

"Think this squirrel's done?" Old Blue said, bringing back my thought to hunger. The young squirrel almost melted in my mouth and the strong black coffee washed it down. I wished we could camp here forever, but tomorrow would bring Old Blue's flock in sight.

Later, I lay rolled in my blanket, staring at the new moon rising over the mountains, pale lemon yellow in its newness. The stars outshone it, big and bright, twinkling so close to the earth it seemed I might touch them.

I thought of my folks again, as I did nearly every night; how the new team Pa was driving home ran away, tumbling the wagon Pa and Ma were in almost straight down a steep mountainside. One of my uncles had found them there. I'd give everything in the world to have them back again, but I knew I never could.

The farm was to have been mine, Papa had told me so often, because I was their only youngun, but the uncles said I was too young. But I wasn't too young to see the greed in their eyes. Fifty acres of good river land and a big sturdy house.

Someday I'll go back, someday when I'm older, and I will claim what is mine. That's one reason I couldn't be Christian. A man of God, like Old Blue, 'cause I might need to kill somebody to get my land back and Christians didn't do that. On that thought, I fell asleep.

We rose with the sun, not building a fire, 'cause we would be at Granny Hassen's place in an hour. We rode side by side because we were nearly on top of the mountain and the land was flatter.

"Blue, iffen thar's a war, will ye go?" I asked over the chopping of the mules' shoes. "Or are ye too old?"

Old Blue looked thoughtful, staring down his beard, then said, "Reckon I'd go iffen they'll let me, but iffen not, reckon I'll stay and look after the old folks and younguns. When a war comes, ever'one is needed, and I think maybe I'm 'bout the only circuit ridin' preacher left, 'less somebody wants to follow in my footsteps." He half grinned. I knew what he was getting at but acted like I didn't hear him. I felt there was no way I could love Old Blue's people the way he did, not ever. Not even if I had been to the mourners' bench.

Granny Hassen's house came in sight. It was made of clapboards, old and faded, sagging in places. It was even a hundred years older than Granny, and she was eighty-three. The house set in an open glen; scrawny chickens scratched in the dirt. There was a well at the end of the sagging porch and a few old lilac bushes trying to bloom. Granny stood on the porch in a long faded dress and an old-fashioned poke bonnet, shading her eyes—which seen only dimly now—with hands covered with brown spots.

As we rode up she called in a high cackling

14

voice, "That be ye, Brother Blue? That be ye and the youngun?"

"Yes, we're heer, Granny," Old Blue called, and we slid down the mules, scattering the chickens.

"Wal, ye git in this heer house," Granny crackled. "Done got your breakfast ready, knowed ye was a-comin' today."

I felt my stomach shrink a little. One thing Old Blue taught me first off was that you never insulted a mountain woman by refusing to put your feet under the table. Most places I was glad to, but Granny was half-blind or more and a body never knew what she would put on your plate. All I knew for sure was that it was never good.

We went slowly into the house, Granny chattering a mile a minute. Her furniture was old, too—real old. Her husband had bought it for her when she was a bride, hauling it up the mountains by wagons and mules. A lot of the stuff was horsehair and wore almost bald. You couldn't tell what color the rugs had been, they were so faded and full of dust. Granny refused to leave the mountains or the home he had brought her to. Old Blue said her younguns had tried to get her to go to the towns where they lived, but she wouldn't budge.

"Now ye all sit down," Granny said, leading us to a kitchen that looked like it had never seen daylight. We sat at an oilcloth-covered table that looked like it hadn't been scrubbed for a hundred years.

15

Granny fumbled around the old wood cookstove, slapping stuff in bowls and setting them before us. My stomach heaved in spite of myself, and I gave Old Blue a pleading look, but he just stared coldly back at me and bowed his head to say one of the long blessings Granny loved.

I stirred the gray mess in my bowl and wished he would pray all day. There were lumps in the bowl, too, lumps of only the Lord knew what. Old Blue raised his head and took a bite, keeping his face frozen straight. There was nothing else I could do, so I decided to take big bites and hurry and get through.

Lord have mercy. It seemed the lump I swallowed came alive, and it was scratching at my throat to get out. "I swallowed somethin', Blue," I whispered. "I done swallowed somethin'."

I felt green and must have looked it, 'cause Old Blue said, "The boy's off his feed, Granny. He'll go and cut ye some wood."

I tried to walk, but my feet wouldn't let me. I ran outside to the back of the house and puked until my belly was clean, and I decided one thing for damn sure. If eating something you didn't like or stuff you didn't even know what it was, was part of a preacher's life, I'd never be one. Not come hell or high water.

Three

When I felt like looking around again, I saw the whole backyard was full of chopped wood, enough to do Granny Hassen a whole spring and summer. I went back into the house where Granny and Old Blue were still sitting at the table and I said, "The yard is already full of cut wood, Blue."

"Oxalee done it," Granny said, tightening her toothless mouth. "That devil came big as brass, Brother Blue. Wouldn't let him step a foot in my door,

17

not that devil. He would have had me a-drinkin' his whiskey iffen I had let him git his big toe in heer. When he left, thar was 'nough wood for winter and a deer and rabbits a-hangin' in the smoke house to freeze. I'll tell ye Brother Blue, I would have been in a pickle iffen I hadn't eat on the meat Oxalee left. I would have starved to death and iffen I hadn't burnt the wood, I would have froze to death, havin' no kin close to help me. So I just kept a-prayin'. Thank ye, Brother Blue, I mean 'bout that devil a-keepin' this old Christian alive."

"Why, Granny, I think the Lord works in wondrous ways," Old Blue said gently.

In a little while Granny said, "That takes a sore load off of my heart, a sore load. Will ye read me some Bible? I jist can't see the words no more."

Old Blue opened his Bible and I shot back outside, feeling I had had enough Bible reading to last me a lifetime. I mean, Old Blue had taught me to read and spell from the Bible. That had started four years ago, and it sure hadn't stopped yet, and I'll be danged if I was going to let Old Blue's Bible reading ruin the enjoyment of my one yearly trip away from home.

I sat on the fallen-down porch and raised my face to the sun, taking deep breaths of the pine-scented air until I was half-asleep, not thinking of anything, just resting.

I nearly jumped off the porch when Old Blue called, "Hambone, come on over heer." I rubbed my

18

eyes and went to the house. "Tell Granny bye and thank her fer the food," Old Blue said, "We best be a-gittin'."

"Thank ye, Granny," I said, though I wasn't thankful at all, and went to get the mules ready. Then Old Blue prayed with Granny one last time before the revival meeting. I was more than eager to get going. I dearly loved stopping at our next place and could hardly wait to fill my belly on good stuff.

Anybody could plainly see that Miss Rosemary loved Old Blue like crazy, I mean anybody 'cept Old Blue. All he could see, seemed to me, was his Bible and the flock of folks he preached to.

Miss Rosemary came to the mountains before I did. She came as a country nurse and stayed on to doctor folks. She helped the folks almost as much as Old Blue did, and she learned her medicine from the old granny women.

There were starched white curtains at the windows, cheerful rag rugs on the floors, and all sorts of herbs drying from the kitchen rafters, and there was always the mouth-watering smell of spices.

Miss Rosemary was setting out some honeysuckles by the front door when we rode up. She came leaning over the gate to smile welcome to us and I just stared my fill at her. She wasn't much taller than me, her hair was gold, her eyes the color of purple pansies. Her lips were as pink as the honeysuckles were, and I felt I could look at her forever.

19

"Come on boy, git down," Old Blue said, nudging me in the ribs. I slid off the mule, feeling my face burn from being caught rudely staring, but Miss Rosemary just smiled at me and said, "Ye folks wash up, I'm jist gittin' lunch on the table."

"Iffen yer shore ye got 'nough," Old Blue said.

Miss Rosemary laughed at him, saying, "And jist when do I ever not have 'nough, Blue, knowin' ye'd be heer the first day of spring?"

Old Blue laughed, too, and we went to wash up in the pan next to the back door. My eyes hungrily surveyed the kitchen—the herbs hanging from the rafters, the copper pots hanging behind the wood stove—and lit to linger on a large pan of gingerbread. There were beans, green ones, canned from her own garden, and venison steaks, thick and juicy, and biscuits dripping with butter. Miss Rosemary had her own cow and reckoned that by mountain standards she was almost rich.

"Good steak," Old Blue said, with a look of pure enjoyment on his face.

"Yes, Sam Horton and his boy, Jeb, brought me a big fat deer this winter."

"Payin' ye fer a-doctorin'," Old Blue grinned.

Miss Rosemary said softly, "They's got no other way of payin', Blue. And iffen they gave me money, I would have to buy food with it anyway. So things worked out very well. But I am worried 'bout most of the folks, Blue. They had a bad winter. Mabel Facker

20

passed away in spite of all I could do. Tom has her in a snowbank till ye come to bury her. He couldn't have buried her this winter even iffen ye had been heer. The ground has been too frozen to dig."

My appetite left me suddenly, thinking of Mabel Facker in a snowbank, but Miss Rosemary was going on: "Reckon they'll be a-weddin' the same day as the funeral. Tom took up with Mazy-June Howard and moved her in with him and the younguns, and now Mazy-June is expectin' and she's only fifteen years old, Blue," Miss Rosemary said sadly. I remembered Mazy-June, a big fat freckled girl with corn-colored hair and sort of dull-looking eyes.

Old Blue said, "Poor child"—shaking his head— "not much of a life fer her, I reckon."

"No, but maybe it was the only chance she had at all fer a life, Blue. Ye know how her pa beat her and the other younguns." Old Blue nodded and Miss Rosemary went on: "Not much more news. I mean, it was a hard winter as usual, a lot of sickness, dyin', and livin'. The Brewer baby was born dead, and Sam Horton is bound and determined to wed Pretty Girl, now it's known she's pregnant, and Sam and Jeb are out to kill the man who did it."

"Is it known who did it?" Old Blue asked.

Miss Rosemary said quickly, "They think, or most folks think, it was Oxalee. I'm not sure."

"Has Oxalee been heer?" Old Blue asked, his voice harsh.

21

"He came by a couple of times," Miss Rose-mary said.

"He give ye any trouble?" Old Blue snapped.

"None that I couldn't handle," Miss Rosemary said quietly, then, after a pause, "This time."

"I think me and Oxalee's a-gonna have to have us a talk 'fore this trip is over," Old Blue said.

I waited for the gingerbread with the thought of the little dead woman in the snowbank in the back of my mind and hated myself for wanting to eat anyway.

Old Blue and Miss Rosemary sat talking for a long while. Once I thought he was holding her hand, but when he seen me looking, he shook it and let it drop. Miss Rosemary turned pink and I left the table to get a drink of water that I didn't even want, wishing Old Blue would wake up and marry her before somebody else did.

When we started to leave, Miss Rosemary said, "I'll meet ye at Tom's tomorrow fer Mabel's funeral and Mazy-June's weddin'."

Old Blue nodded and shook her hand again. Miss Rosemary hugged me and she smelt like lilacs. I felt like I could stand with her arms around me all day, but Blue dragged me away.

I didn't care if we got to Tom Facker's place or not, and I kept my eyes turned away from every snowbank we passed just in case there was a body in it. I hated Tom and Mazy-June both for living snug and warm while Mabel lay cold in the snow. I had liked Mabel; she was small and worked herself half to death, but she always had a smile for me and a biscuit with honey.

Tom's house was sort of spread down the mountainside, one small room after another, tacked on as more younguns came into the world. I never really got a count on the kids, but Old Blue said Tom and Mabel had a dozen at least, and now Mazy-June, just fifteen, was in the birthin' way and Lord knows how many she might have, maybe another dozen or two.

A couple of towheaded boys, about ten and twelve, came to put the mules in the barn, and Tom came to the door to welcome us, saying, "Ye heerd 'bout Mabel, Preacher?"

Old Blue nodded sadly, then said dryly, "I heard 'bout Mazy-June, too."

"A man has to comfort himself, Preacher," Tom said, his face red and his voice sort of 'shamed and mad all at the same time.

"Seems thar's times a man can wait fer his comfort," Old Blue said.

Tom's face went redder and he said grouchily, "Mazy-June was brought to me when work got out of control after Mabel's passin'. She was brought to my house and I reckon I got a right to my comfort, same as any man. 'Sides, I got a whole passel of younguns that need a woman's hand."

"Who brought Mazy-June to ye, Tom?" Old Blue asked quietly.

"Oxalee," Tom answered.

Somehow, I didn't think me or Old Blue, either, was surprised.

Four

The house was full of crawling babies and bigger kids just a few years older. Puppies tumbled around with the little ones, so a body had to be careful where he stepped.

Mazy-June came out of the kitchen, wiping her hands on her apron. She looked different to me and it took me a while to see the reason why. She wasn't dull anymore. I mean, her eyes. She was grinning all over her face, saying, "Make yerself at home, Preacher. Ye younguns and doggies, git! Git, ye heer me?" And the kids scattered out of her way as she led us to the kitchen table.

She poured coffee for Old Blue and Tom, saying, "Wal, Preacher, I guess ye heard me and Tom is a-gonna wed soon as Mabel's in the ground. I know it seemed we was a-hurryin' a mite, but I had to git out of the house. Pa was a-beatin' me ag'in. A-beatin' me fierce. Oxalee happened by and seen Pa a-beatin' me. He took the belt away from Pa and whipped him hard with it. Boy, Preacher, ye outta heerd how Pa bellowed. Made me feel plum good," Mazy-June laughed real cheerful, her big face turning red with pleasure.

Old Blue's eyes were sort of dancing, but he kept his face straight. I didn't; I grinned all over. I mean, I sort of admired Oxalee, 'cause I had heard a lot of tales about how mean Mazy-June's pa was to his younguns.

"Oxalee told Pa he was a-gonna come and whip him ever' time he heerd Pa had beat on Ma or one of the other younguns," Mazy-June went on. "And Pa knows, like ever'body else, that Oxalee does what he says. Anyway, Preacher, Oxalee brought me heer, said Tom needed a woman and heer I be," she laughed again, her big stomach shaking, but I stopped laughing when I thought of Mabel lying in the snowbank.

Somehow, the day passed in a haze with barking dogs and squalling younguns. Big ones helped wait on the table as Mazy-June cooked a huge pot of beans and a pile of corn bread.

After supper, Tom pushed his chair away from the table and said, "Wal, Preacher, reckon it's time to bring Mabel in fer her last night at home."

It seemed like my blood froze and it was hard for me to breathe. I was so afraid Old Blue or Tom would ask me to help, but they didn't.

They were gone a long time, and when they did come in, they were carrying a homemade pine coffin. They carried it into the living room and set it on sawhorses. A feeling of relief flooded me; for some reason I thought Mabel had been lying in the snowbank, naked and cold.

Tom made all the younguns go look at her, but I wouldn't and Old Blue didn't say I had to. I knew he would set beside the coffin all night and read his Bible by an oil lamp.

Tom and Mazy-June bedded me down with the biggest boys, but I couldn't sleep because they kept crying deep inside. Then the smaller ones were whimpering in their sleep. I cried, too, but real quiet so nobody could hear. I felt sorry for the younguns. I mean, I would have been half-crazy if my mama had lain in the snowbank all winter.

Soon rain started beating on the tin roof in one of the sudden mountain storms and the boys cried themselves to sleep one by one until the only sound was the rain on the roof.

I missed my folks fierce. I slipped from the bed, and, coffin or not, I went to find Old Blue. I needed somebody alive. He was sitting in a rocking chair, his Bible open in the lamplight, but he wasn't reading.

I dropped down on the floor beside him, saying gruffly, "Thought ye might need company, Blue." Then I said bitterly, "It ought to be Tom a-sittin' heer, 'stead of ye."

"Wal, reckon he has had all winter to git used to Mabel a-bein' gone, boy. So don't judge too harsh."

" 'Tis jist like Mabel meant nothin' to him a'tall," I said in despair, trying to make Old Blue understand me.

"Wal, I reckon he did jump the gun by a long shot," Old Blue said kindly. "But remember, he had all those younguns to care fer."

"I don't care what he has. 'Tis no excuse," I said stubbornly. "I can sorta understand Mazy-June, her pa a-beatin' her and all, but not Tom, Blue." And without knowing I was going to, I walked over to the coffin and stared down at Mabel's small face. She just looked asleep, but somehow not tired anymore.

Old Blue's voice came gently: "Mabel's past carin' fer the cares of this world, boy. Knowin' Mabel, she would be right glad to have someone a-lookin' after her younguns. Now, I don't abide Tom's a-takin' Mazy-June to wed afore time, but he did, and we have to think on the good side, like the younguns a-havin' a ma and Mazy-June not a-gittin' beat anymore."

I didn't understand, but I nodded and took one last look at the small peaceful face. When I went back to bed, I didn't dream; I just let the raindrops lull me to sleep, not thinking at all.

The house was quiet the next morning, even the babies and puppies were quiet. The rain had passed over and the sun shone bright. There was a nice nip in the air and I fed our mules. When I got back to the house, Mazy-June had fed the kids and their faces wore a fresh-scrubbed look. Maybe Old Blue was right, I mean about Mazy-June being good for the younguns.

Soon Miss Rosemary pulled up in her old car, and Old Blue and Tom nailed down the coffin and loaded it on Tom's pickup. I rode with Miss Rosemary and the younguns sat in the back of the pickup around the coffin.

We rode to the graveyard a few miles up the mountainside. The road was narrow and bumpy, but all the mountain roads were. You couldn't even get a car up the mountains the way Old Blue and I came. That's why we rode mules—not that we had a car, but I wished for one. Old Blue said it would be more trouble that it was worth on the rough old roads.

There were just a few tombstones and wooden crosses in the old cemetery. Seemed like mountain people just lived longer. A new grave was dug under a pine, looking raw and red from the clay mixed with the soil.

We all gathered around while Old Blue read from the Bible. He talked about what a good woman Mabel was. I figured Tom must have been up before daybreak to have the grave ready.

I drew my mind back to Old Blue, who was saying, "A stranger never came to Mabel's door that she didn't feed and make walcome. She gave all herself to others and I never did heer her complain. She loved the Lord and proved it by living daily in kindness."

I stared at Tom to see if he was going to cry. His face looked stern as a rock, but beside him, fat Mazy-June sobbed softly and the younguns sniffed in their sleeves, their towheads shining in the sun. Miss Rosemary's tears ran slowly down her face, but she made no sound.

Old Blue bowed his head and prayed, "Lord, heer this, one of Yer children has come home and I know her walcome was a joy. Help us to remember Mabel's kindness when we would be harsh in our judgments. Amen."

Old Blue, Tom, and I lowered the coffin in the ground. Then Tom and the bigger boys filled the grave. When it was done, the younguns seemed to feel free, moving around and talking among themselves, the baby ones fretting to go home.

Miss Rosemary and I drove back to the house, and I said, "Did ye leave all them spring flowers next to Mabel's grave?"

"No," she said softly, "but I can guess who it was."

"Who?" I asked curiously.

"Why, Oxalee, of course." She smiled a little.

"But folks sez he's a devil," I protested.

"Maybe," Miss Rosemary said quietly, and I said no more.

The house buzzed with noise and I felt sad. I mean it was sort of like Mabel had never been there at all. Mazy-June's fat laugh sounded above the youn-guns and puppies; Tom even looked cheerful. He and Mazy-June stood beside the fireplace while Old Blue read the wedding vows, holding the Bible, and it seemed like it was over in no time flat. Mazy-June pulled two egg cakes out of the cupboard and Miss Rosemary gave us each a piece.

After awhile, Miss Rosemary, Old Blue, and I walked to her car, Old Blue saying, "Iffen the war comes, and it sure looks like it, will ye go home, Rosemary?"

"This is my home now," Miss Rosemary said quietly. "When the war comes, my people will need me; the young, the old, and the wives left behind."

"I feel that way, too," Old Blue said. "Wal, reckon we'll see ye at the revival, Rosemary."

"I would never miss it, Blue." She laughed, and the smile faded as she said, "This might be our last revival, iffen the war does come."

Old Blue nodded and I felt half-mad at him for letting her go without any soft words. It was so plain to see she loved him.

"So, go git the mules, boy. We best be a-gittin' on our way," Old Blue said.

I thought hatefully, "Hey hi, hey hi ho, Old Blue Tilley's a-gonna save some souls."

Five

It was a long ride to Sam Horton's place, but it was sort of nice. The spring air was almost warm and the snowdrifts were melting under the pines and cedars. The mountain air made me half-starved and I hoped Sam or his boy, Jeb, was a good cook.

There were no women in their house; nobody talked about it much. Sam's wife and Jeb's mama, Serie, had run off with a peddling man a couple years ago. I tried to talk to Old Blue about it, but he said sharply that it was none of my business, or his, for that matter. It was between Sam and his Serie and he couldn't say anything unless they came to him and they never did.

It was dark by the time we got to the house built of mountain rock. A long, low gray rock house that set under pines that seemed to sing sad songs day and night. I didn't like the place—I felt uneasy in it—but it looked cheerful enough inside with the leaping, crackling fire in the rock fireplace. The house was sort of messy, but not dirty.

Sam and Jeb shooed dogs away from the fire and led Old Blue and me to the chairs. My mouth watered because the house smelt like baking ham and sweet potatoes. I kept looking at Sam, but he lit his pipe and settled down to talk to Old Blue.

Sam was a tall, dark man who looked mad all the time, but his voice was friendly whenever he talked, which wasn't much. Jeb was big, too, but he had gold hair and blue eyes like Serie's.

I gave a sigh of regret that we weren't eating and settled down in my chair to listen. I mean Old Blue said I was nosy, but for the life of me I couldn't figure nothing else to do but listen. A body just didn't get up and wander about someone else's house.

My ears perked up because Sam was saying heavily, "Oxalee got to Pretty Girl, Blue. Jeb heer was a-gonna wed her, but he can't have a woman that's been touched."

34

"Don't want her now," Jeb muttered bitterly.

"But I'll kill Oxalee fer it, Blue, 'cause he knows my boy had his mark on her," Sam said, sounding mean, and I had a sudden fear for Oxalee.

"Ain't a family in these mountains he ain't touched," Sam went on.

When he paused, I blurted, "He done chopped Granny Hassen's wood and killed her a deer fer winter meat."

Sam turned such a hateful look on me that I shrunk back in the chair, and he said, "Ye ought to teach that youngun to be seen and not heerd, Blue. And not seen no more than he can help it."

Old Blue sort of grinned at me, 'cause he knew I was too scared to open my mouth again. Sam went on, "Womenfolks ain't no good, Blue. I done told Jeb so, but he would'da had Pretty Girl, and now look, she falls down fer the first man in long britches."

"She's only sixteen, Sam," Old Blue said gently. "And since she never spoke a word in her life, a body can't rightly blame her."

"No woman is good, Blue," Sam said, "and iffen Jeb don't shoot Oxalee, I will."

As if Old Blue hadn't heard Sam, he said, "Iffen it's true, and he is the youngun's pa, I think he ought to and will marry Pretty Girl, iffen I have anythin' to say 'bout it. But, Sam, are ye right shore Oxalee done it?"

"Shore as I am that Oxalee is bound for hell,"

Sam snapped. "Ever'time I took Jeb to court Pretty Girl, she run away to Oxalee's, and after we left, Oxalee would bring her back to her mama. Her mama told us so."

Old Blue shook his head sadly; I looked at Jeb. He seemed excited, then blurted, "Brother Blue, I'm a-gonna join the army after revival time, now that Pretty Girl's been touched. I can't see nothin' to stay heer fer."

"Ye still have yer pa and the land, boy," Old Blue said.

"I know," Jeb said stubbornly. "That's why I'm gonna fight, for Pa, the land, and our neighbors. I mean, somebody has to fight fer the old and the young and their pas. Roosevelt will declare war on Germany 'fore long, and I'm a-gonna go early 'cause I think a body outta be a jump ahead."

"Ye may be right, Jeb, but I hate to see our young men goin' to war," Old Blue said, and Sam nodded in sober agreement, but Jeb's eyes were dancing like he couldn't hardly wait and I figured Pretty Girl wasn't setting heavy on his mind at all.

Seemed like I was dying of hunger when Sam finally rose and led us to the stone-floored kitchen. There was ham baked in a candied coat of molasses and sweet potatoes, beans and pickles. For a little while, I felt pure content.

After supper, I helped Jeb wash the dishes and carry in the morning wood, then tumbled thankfully into the warm bed they gave me, leaving Old Blue and Sam to talk half the night away.

The wind in the pine trees sounded like it was crying, and I wondered what it would be like living with that sound day after day, and if that was why Serie didn't live here anymore. I thought maybe Sam and Jeb wouldn't like women much anymore. I mean, since Serie left and Pretty Girl being touched by Oxalee. I fell asleep and dreamed I was crying.

It was daybreak when we rode away from the sighing, crying pines, and I thought Sam Horton's place must be the loneliest place in the whole world. But that didn't keep me from eating all the biscuits I could hold, because from now on we would be visiting the poorest of Old Blue's flock and we would be lucky to eat at all. I mean, unless we could kill some squirrels or rabbits. The deer stayed too far up the mountains this time of year.

The path we rode down was so steep, I kept trying to slide off my mule because the folks we were going to see lived in a valley between the mountains. Pretty Girl and her ma would be our first stop.

Pretty Girl's ma was almost paper thin, her lips bitter, her eyes hungry. Her man had left her and Pretty Girl years before, gone away to the city, some folks said.

Pretty Girl was just that, the prettiest girl the mountains and valley had ever seen. Her hair was so black, it had a blue shine and her skin was pure cream with a hint of pink in her cheeks. I could stare at her eyes all day; they were purple, sort of lilac purple. I had never seen eyes like that before and Old Blue couldn't recall seeing that color, either.

Pretty Girl couldn't talk, but she wasn't dumb. Miss Rosemary had taught her to read and she could write notes when she wanted to talk. I didn't much admire Oxalee now that he had touched Pretty Girl. I felt mad and sad at the same time. I mean, Oxalee was an old man, old as Old Blue, least ways, forty or forty-five, and it seemed to me a shame that an old dirty man should touch Pretty Girl. I sighed long and deep that Oxalee was a pure mess. All over the mountains and valley, he left his mark everywhere.

I rode up to Old Blue's side, saying, "Blue, do ye think Oxalee will go to war?"

"Ye asked me that 'fore," Old Blue said, "and I jist don't know. Oxalee is always in the middle of his own war, some kind or other." He sort of laughed.

"That old man, he ain't got no business touching Pretty Girl," I said bitterly.

Old Blue gave me a shrewd look, saying, "I reckon all men want to be the first one to touch a girl and most men would fight to be the first if it's a girl they like or love. Fact of the matter, boy, reckon most men only feel themselves as worthy of touching the ones they want for the first time."

I felt my face go red, 'cause I have been wishing that Pretty Girl would have waited to be touched by

38

me when I got older. I felt angry at Old Blue and said, "Oxalee is a dirty old man."

"We will have to leave Oxalee fer God to judge, that's what I reckon, Hambone," Old Blue said. "But ye, Jeb, and Sam talk like Pretty Girl is dead or worse, jist 'cause she's been touched. But it ain't so; she's alive, she feels, she gits hungry jist like ye do. God still loves her, she's still Pretty Girl. Now boy, I ain't a-sayin' it's right that Oxalee touched her, if he did without wedlock. Till we know fer shore, we best not judge too harsh; let me ask ye somethin' boy, would ye have felt better iffen it had been Jeb who touched Pretty Girl?"

"Nobody outta touch Pretty Girl," I snapped.

Old Blue said gently, "Maybe till ye git 'round to it, huh?"

I didn't answer him, just kicked my mule ahead of his and rode on down the trail. I hated when Old Blue seemed to know how I felt before I did.

Sunbeams danced between the trees, which had new green buds on them. Little waterfalls leaked down the mountainsides, hurrying to their mother river in the valley. A body would think with the river and bottom land, folks living there would be well off, but they were poor as field mice and most all of them lived off what fish they could catch. My pa and ma did good on their river bottomland and reckon my old greedy uncle was doing the same. I gave a deep sigh, wishing my folks had just lived.

39

Crops didn't seem to grow along this bottom-land and hardly a spring passed that the river didn't flood, its banks washing away nigh all the folks around, and I couldn't understand why folks kept building back instead of moving farther up the mountain so the floods wouldn't reach them. Sometimes it seemed 'most everything was plumb beyond me.

Pretty Girl and her ma lived in a shack that sort of leaned to one side. It was faded almost silver with boards that had never seen paint, but it was high enough to be out of the floodwater way. A few straggly chickens scratched in the grassless, flowerless yard, and a skinny calico cat lay in the sun on the small porch.

Pretty Girl's ma stood at the gate, saying, "Ye jist git in heer, Brother Blue. Ye jist git in heer," which meant we were welcome.

I was hungry again because the sun was past noon, but I didn't expect to eat much here, and that was just as well for I didn't smell anything cooking when we followed Pretty Girl's ma into the house. The place was spotless clean, the wood floor was polished white with sand, and even the old rock fireplace gleamed.

We sat on two straight chairs and Pretty Girl's ma chattered tight-lipped, "Ye heer 'bout Pretty Girl and Oxalee, Brother Blue?"

"Ye shore it's Oxalee's, Ma?" Blue asked.

40

"Shore as I'm a-sittin' heer, Brother Blue. Oxalee hung 'round this house all winter. I thought he was a-courtin' me," she said bitterly, her little eyes snapping. "He brought us squirrels and rabbits, and at Christmas a wild turkey that ye know as well as me it's ag'in the law to kill. He was always a-choppin' wood, always a-tellin' me and Pretty Girl to eat and eat, that he would bring us some more. Sit heer at night, his toes pointed at the fire, sipping from his whiskey jug. Thought it was me he was a-courtin', Blue. Thought it was me."

"Then Pretty Girl got to actin' strange, ever'time Sam Horton brought his boy Jeb over, Pretty Girl ran to Oxalee's place. She didn't fool me long, Brother Blue," she said hatefully, "nor that Oxalee, neither. It was when Pretty Girl started losing her vitals, then I knew." Her voice dropping to a low wail, she said, "Thought he was a-courtin' me, Brother Blue."

When she was quiet, Old Blue patted her hand, his eyes sad, and for some reason I felt sorry and didn't really know why, except I knew I would take Pretty Girl over her ma any day.

Six

Before I could think on it any further, the door flew open and Pretty Girl came in with a big string of fish. My mouth watered; I loved fish, but it was Pretty Girl I couldn't keep from staring at.

She smiled at us and it seemed like spring flowers had walked in the room with her. I could see pieces of paper sticking out of her blue-jean pockets. She always carried them since Miss Rosemary had taught her to read and write. Miss Rosemary said

Pretty Girl was one of the smartest in the hills.

In the background, I could hear Pretty Girl's ma going on to Old Blue in a high whining voice. I followed Pretty Girl outside to help her clean the fish. I never felt the need to talk to her, mostly I just wanted to look at her. We laughed as fish scales flew around over our faces. We washed the fish in the river and cut them in slices.

Pretty Girl's ma was still talking to Old Blue a mile a minute when we went back in. It was Pretty Girl and I who cooked, rolling the fish in cornmeal and frying it in hog lard until it was crunchy brown. We fried potatoes, too, and Pretty Girl made corn bread.

After we ate, I helped Pretty Girl clean the dishes. When I noticed anything besides Pretty Girl again, it was to see Old Blue kneeling beside his chair and Pretty Girl's ma praying. Her prayers sounded like she was mad at God; she kept yelling for Him to send Oxalee to hell right then.

Old Blue's prayer was just a gentle murmur. When he finished we would ride on to the Davises', because Old Blue said it wasn't proper for menfolks to stay in a manless home.

I went outside, but Pretty Girl was gone so I sat in the sun until Old Blue came out, thinking about the Davises, who lived far down the valley, and about Clem mostly. Miss Rosemary said Clem was even smarter than people who had gone to college. Miss

Rosemary had even made special trips to the town library miles and miles away to get Clem books. Clem, like everyone else, had never been to school. I thought maybe Miss Rosemary was the best blessing the mountain and valley folks ever had.

All of us folks were poor, I reckoned. I mean, nobody had money, but most of us raised enough food to eat or hunted it. But I reckoned the Davises were the poorest, along with some of the other valley folks. Most people said they were trashy and shiftless, but though I might have thought it myself once in a while, I'd never say it out loud, for Old Blue would strip the hide from me. Old Blue loved all his people and if a body insulted them, they insulted Old Blue, too.

I liked Clem Davis a lot. He was nigh twenty and he couldn't help not working because he had a leg that was twisted bad and he had to use a crutch to walk. Miss Rosemary said it was a birth defect. There were a lot of birth defects in the valley. Miss Rosemary said it was from kin marrying kin. I mean, I would hear her tell Old Blue that and they didn't know I was listening. I knew one thing, if I was old enough to wed, Pretty Girl was the only girl in the valley I would have, even if she had been touched.

It was midafternoon when we came to the Davises' place. The house was just a long, low shack, leaning to the side like Pretty Girl's place, like it would fall over any moment. There wasn't a touch of paint any place and the grassless yard was full of kids in ages from crawling to teens, all barefoot and ragged.

Old man Davis sat in a broken-down rocker on the porch, dressed in bib overalls that his dirty gray beard just touched. Tobacco juice had dried in streams down his beard and he sipped from a jug, peering at us over the top with his little black eyes.

A sudden picture of my own pa flashed in my mind. Pa was a tall, clean, and laughing man; a fierce longing for my own folks came over me, and I wondered what Clem Davis thought of his pa, this dirty, drunk old man.

Then the picture went away, because the old man was speaking: "So ye got heer, Preacher." Old Blue nodded and the old man went on, "Reckon the wife and younguns will walcome ye, but ye ain't got no walcome from me. I always hated preachers, always will. A-pokin' thar noses whare it don't belong. Ain't never had no trouble with God, never will. I decided a long time ago, I wouldn't bother Him iffen He wouldn't bother me. Waste of time, preachers always a-sayin', 'Don't, don't, don't.' Don't do thin's that makes a body happy. Like whiskey, tomcattin', and dancin' music. No, ye ain't a-gittin' a walcome from me, Blue Tilley. Now that Oxalee, he understands a man and what a man wonts."

"That's whare Pa gets his jug," Clem Davis said, as he hobbled out on the porch, dragging his crip-

45

pled leg and holding a book in his hand. Clem was tall. His worn-out clothes were as clean as a washing could make them, his eyes blue, his hair gold. Old Blue shook hands with him and I returned his smile; plenty of welcome there. In the background, old man Davis's voice whined on, but we paid him no mind and soon he droned on to a drunken sleep.

Mrs. Davis came out, followed by a pack of younguns. She was a skinny, lean woman with stringy, brownish gray hair and tired lines around her faded blue eyes and mouth. She was a lot younger than old man Davis and her belly was big awaiting birth.

"Yer a welcome sight, Blue Tilley," she said, holding out a bony hand for him to shake, and he done so very gently, his eyes full of love and compassion. Nodding toward her husband, she said ashamedly, "Oxalee's done been heer, Blue. Jist overlook him." Old Blue nodded, then smiled at all the younguns and patted their heads.

"I'll jist go and cook us up some supper," Mrs. Davis said, and Old Blue and I followed Clem to some broken-down chairs at the end of the porch away from the old man's snores.

We sat down and Clem looked at Old Blue, his eyes clouded. "I am really glad yer heer, Blue," he said. "I am worried 'bout Ma. She's not actin' right, not like the other times she birthed. This youngun makes her twelfth, and Miss Rosemary said she

46

shouldn't have anymore. But ye know Pa, Ma didn't have a chance. 'Tis past time fer her birthin', Blue. The rest of us do what we can to help her, but I'm not much use," he said bitterly, looking at his twisted leg.

"Yer a big help to yer ma jist a-bein' heer," Old Blue said gently.

"I'm more trouble than ye know, Blue," Clem said, still bitter.

So I jumped in saying, "Ye got any new books, Clem?"

His face lightened up and he replied, "Miss Rosemary brought me 'nough to last the winter. Trouble is, I have a hard time to keep from gobblin' them all up at once." He grinned, then said, "I don't know what these hills would do without Miss Rosemary. I aim to send fer her when Ma's time comes. 'Tis a comfort to know she'll come." Both Old Blue and I nodded.

We were quiet for a long time, then Clem said, "I want to marry, Blue. I want to marry Pretty Girl, but I don't see how I can." Despair was plain in his voice, "Jist look at this pig sty, Brother Blue, and there is not enough money to set up housekeepin' on our own. 'Sides, I can't work, jist look at me. I don't understand how Pretty Girl could love me at all. And now, God forgive me, she's a-gonna have my child."

"Anybody know this but ye?" Old Blue asked sharply.

47

Clem shook his head sadly, then said, "No, un-less it's Oxalee. He had seen us a-walkin' in the woods a few times."

"Try not to suffer so bad, boy," Old Blue said, and laid a gentle hand on Clem's shoulder. "Maybe we can think of somethin' betwixt us. Course, ye know, ye have to wed Pretty Girl 'fore long. Youn-guns got a way of not waitin' till folks make up thar minds."

Before more could be said, one of the tow-headed girls came running out on the porch, crying, "Clem, Clem. Ma's took bad!"

"Will yer car run, boy?" Old Blue snapped, pointing to a beat-up old pickup.

"I keep it goin'," Clem said quietly.

"Then go git Miss Rosemary and hurry. Ham-bone, ye git to heatin' water," Old Blue said, taking off his coat and going into the house.

All sizes of younguns came to help, their eyes wide, their voices quiet. I felt sorry for them; they looked skinny and half-starved.

We drew water from a well near the back porch and some of the bigger boys cut wood and built a fire in the cookstove, and we set the two washtubs full of water to heat.

I could hear low groans coming from one of the bedrooms. On the porch, old man Davis slept on, snoring drunkenly. I didn't like that old man at all and couldn't for the life of me figure out what Old

Blue meant by saying, "We should love ever'one, even iffen we didn't like them. We should love thar souls." I just couldn't see nothing to love about old man Davis and felt mean at Oxalee for letting him have whiskey.

A sharp scream came from the bedroom, making me jump and look fearfully over my shoulder toward the door. Two of the oldest girls herded the younger ones outside and I figured they had been through this birthing thing before. I didn't know what else to do, so I went back out and sat on the porch watching the river roll by at the end of the yard, wondering why in the world anybody would build so close to it when they were bound to be flooded during the spring mountain snowfall.

One of the older boys was fishing with a cane pole with a can of worms by his side. I watched him pull in a seven- or eight-pound catfish and put it on a stringer with the others, and I knew that would be our supper. All the valley folks lived mostly on fish.

Little yelling sounds came steadily from the bedroom, making me nervous and jumpy, and I nearly jumped out of my chair when old man Davis opened his blurry eyes and said, "Ye one of mine, boy?" I shook my head in denial and he said, "Didn't think so. All mine got cotton hair. Wal, no matter, my jug's dry. Go fetch me one, it's under my bed."

I shook my head stubbornly, "Mrs. Davis is in thare havin' a youngun."

"Ain't got nothin' to do with my jug, boy. Bring it heer."

I shook my head again. The old man's face turned red and I said, "Ye ain't supposed to drink while yer wife's birthin'."

"Now jist how the hell do ye know what a man's supposed to do?" the old man sputtered. "I drunk all my younguns in this world, and a couple of 'em out of it, too, and ain't no snot-nose youngun a-gonna change my mind. Ye aimin' to be a preacher like Old Blue?" I shook my head and he went on, "Then go git my jug!"

"I ain't allowed in that bedroom," I said. "The other younguns can't go in thare, either. Old Blue said so. Ye have to go yerself."

"I ain't a-gonna go in thare to watch an old woman hug her belly and screech, but I wont my jug."

"Then, I guess yer out of luck," I said real smugly.

"Jist go to the door and tell Blue to hand ye the jug," he insisted.

"Nope." I shook my head.

"Ye need a cane pole took to yer hide!" he yelled.

"And ye need a dip in the river to clean up and sober up," I yelled back at him.

"Aw, come on, boy. Fetch me the jug." He whined now.

"I ain't a-gonna git ye that jug, no matter what

50

ye do or say," I said through my teeth. "Ye ain't got no right to sit heer drunk while Mrs. Davis is a-hurtin'."

"And ye ain't got no right to tell me what to drink," he said, and before I could say more, Clem pulled up in the yard with Miss Rosemary beside him.

Seven

It seemed to me Miss Rosemary made the world a sane place to be—my world at least. She came out of the pickup carrying a bag that I knew was full of medicine and said in a no-nonsense voice, "Hambone, go fix supper fer the younguns, the girls will help ye," and turning to Clem, "Ye see the boys keep plenty of wood cut and the fire a-goin'," and glaring at old man Davis, she snapped, "Ye stay sober!

"Can't help it," he whimpered, "My jug's under

the old woman's bed and nobody will fetch it fer me."

"Good!" Miss Rosemary said firmly, and went through the door.

I could hear Mrs. Davis moaning and Old Blue and Miss Rosemary talking in low voices. Then I was 'most too busy to notice anything 'cause the real little younguns were hanging around the kitchen, fretting and crying for their supper.

I peeled potatoes to fry and one of the bigger boys brought in a mess of clean fish. One of the girls made corn bread and it was a whirlwind until I had the younguns sitting to eat. Then it took the rest of the time to pick bones out of the fish for the babies.

Clem came in and made a big black pot full of coffee, cursing a little 'cause it emptied the coffee can. I figured it would be quite a spell before there was more coffee in that house.

I helped clean the kitchen after supper, 'cause Miss Rosemary was a stickler for things being clean. The moaning from the bedroom was a steady drone in my ears. Old man Davis didn't eat, just whined for his jug every time anyone went near him. Clem didn't eat, either; just paced the floor, back and forth, back and forth, dragging his crippled leg.

Somehow a bed was found for all of us but Old Blue and Miss Rosemary. They wouldn't sleep, I knew; they never did when somebody was sick. I thought I wouldn't sleep, either, but I did, though I woke up every now and then. Once, it was after midnight, and Mrs. Davis seemed to be screaming little sharp screams.

I got up again to use the outhouse, and the same new moon was big in the sky, casting dark shadows. On the way back, I heard voices on the porch and slipped out to stand quietly as Miss Rosemary and Old Blue talked in low tones.

Old Blue was saying, "Rosemary, do ye think Mrs. Davis will make it?"

She answered in a sad voice, "Not 'less the Lord gives her strength, Blue. She's already wore out from childbearin'. Those are twins, no doubt 'bout it. There are two heartbeats."

"I pray God will strengthen her," Old Blue said. "Thare's so many heer that needs a mother and they have no father to speak of. Course, thare's Clem, but he has a load of trouble of his own."

"I'm glad ye told me 'bout Clem and Pretty Girl, Blue. I've been thinkin' 'bout them," Miss Rosemary said. "Ye know how badly we need a school heer, and Clem is capable of teachin', least up to the eighth grade. And thare is a house empty not far from me and Granny Hassen's that Clem and Pretty Girl could rent fer almost nothin'. I'll speak to the county board 'bout it the next time I'm in town."

"God bless ye, Rosemary," Old Blue said gently. "I have been rackin' my brain to help them two and I couldn't think of a thin'. Ye have the right idea with this war comin' and all of our young men goin'; I'd like to think of Clem bein' with the younguns."

"When the war starts, Blue, I don't think thare will be any of our people left but the very old and the very young," Miss Rosemary said sadly. "I think the others will go to town fer the work."

I felt tears and closed my eyes and slipped back to my bed. I lay for a long time looking at the moon shadows on the walls. Mrs. Davis's yelping sounds sounded like a very old and tired dog, and I wondered why it hurt to bring younguns into the world, and if it hurt so bad, why did people have so many? I thought if I ever wed, there would be no children for me and my wife. I wouldn't want a wife of mine to hurt and I would never drink whiskey like old man Davis did, even if Oxalee tried to pour it down my throat.

I couldn't understand Oxalee at all. He did good things, like hunting for meat for the people who had none and keeping old people like Granny Hassen warm during the blue, cold winters, yet he made and sold whiskey to men like old man Davis, who would drink and let his family starve. I didn't understand at all, and I wondered what would happen when Old Blue and Oxalee met at the revival. A sudden excitement shot through me. It would sure be a meeting I wouldn't want to miss.

The sky was lighting with dawn when Mrs. Davis's yelps grew into loud, hair-raising screams. I tried pulling the covers over my head, but it didn't help. All of the younguns started stirring in their beds, some crying. I could hear Clem dragging around the kitchen between the screams and got up to join him. But just as I came in the room, the screams stopped and it was dead quiet; Clem's face turned white as he stared at his mother's door.

Then there was the sound of *slap, slap* and the crying voices of two babies and Old Blue's voice, full of cheerful happiness and thankfulness, saying, "Praise God, Rosemary. Praise God." Miss Rosemary was laughing like she and Old Blue had whipped a wildcat and come out without a scratch.

After a while, everyone tiptoed in to see the babies, me, too. I had never seen twins before. I thought they were ugly, all red and wrinkled, but Miss Rosemary kept saying they were beautiful. I looked curiously at Mrs. Davis; she looked little and tired but had a happy look on her face. I wondered how it could be so.

Old man Davis was the last one to come in. For some reason he looked ashamed of himself and slunk in like an egg-sucking hound dog. He touched each baby with a not-very-clean finger and touched Mrs. Davis on the cheek and a sort of shock went through me when she smiled gently at him. Seems to me she ought to hate him or something.

Suddenly the old man slumped and I thought he

was going to kiss Mrs. Davis. Instead, he stood up with a jug in his hand and a look of smugness on his face. "Got it!" He cackled. "Ye all wouldn't help me, but I got it anyway," he said, looking at me. I would have liked to take it and pound his head in with it, but I didn't say nothing at all and neither did anyone else, not even when he cackled again, and said, "I ain't old, Blue, ye old preacher. I'm a-gittin' two at a time now. No sirree, I ain't old yet." He took his jug and headed for the porch, leaving a shamed silence behind.

After a while Old Blue broke the silence, saying, "Hambone, ye and the younguns git yerselves fed."

I was glad to leave the room and as I left I heard Miss Rosemary telling Blue she would stay with Mrs. Davis a few days longer. I could hardly wait to leave the Davis place. I mean, before the old man got drunk again and I cussed him or something. I said as much to Old Blue as we rode along and blurted, "I don't see how Mrs. Davis and the younguns stand that old man."

"And I'll tell ye ag'in, boy, not to judge too harsh," Old Blue said. "I reckon some folks got out and whipped life and life whipped other folks 'fore they got started good. Maybe that's what happened to Mr. Davis."

"Wal, Oxalee must be mean clear to his toes, a-sellin' that old man whiskey."

"Now yer a-judgin' ag'in, boy. I reckon they ain't hardly a person in this whole world that's all bad or all good."

"Ye shore look at thin's funny, Blue. Do ye think it's right fer Oxalee to sell whiskey to men like old man Davis?"

"No, I don't think it's right," Old Blue said, "On the other hand, I don't see Oxalee twistin' no man's arm or holdin' a gun on him to make him drink it neither. And I'll tell ye somethin' else, boy, iffen a man wonts a drink bad enough, he'll find it someplace, somehow."

I guess I looked sort of mad, 'cause Old Blue kicked his mule ahead and called over his shoulder, "Come on, boy. We got folks to see and a revival to start. Hey hi, hey hi ho!"

Eight

I liked going to Dory and Charles Prince's house. It was built out of mountain stone and high enough above the river so it wouldn't flood. Charles was a big, tall man, with no hair at all on his head, and Dory looked like a dumpling with dimples, always laughing and fixing good things to eat.

Charles played the fiddle and sang at our revivals, but I don't think he would have gone to our church, even if there had been one near enough for him to go to. He and Old Blue didn't believe the same at all. Charles and Dory were the first Catholics I'd ever heard tell of—not that they preached about it or tried to get us to be Catholics, they just didn't talk about their religion so Old Blue didn't talk about his, either. They just enjoyed each other's company and let it go at that.

Charles and Dory had been city people once, years ago, and they were still considered "new people" by valley and mountain folks alike. Nobody knew where they got their money to live on and, though they wondered, no one asked.

Dory and Miss Rosemary were fast friends and Dory often went with Miss Rosemary on her calls to the sick. Miss Rosemary told Old Blue the sight of Dory's cheerful face was better than medicine in some cases and I believed it, 'cause she sure made me feel good.

Everything in Dory's house was starched, ironed, and spotless clean, from the red checkered curtains on the windows to the matching tablecloth. There were braided rugs on the floors, open oak beams, and a leaping fire in the rock fireplace.

But what struck my gaze was a four-layer cake on the table with egg-white frosting, and I knew I'd keep staring at it until I got some. I mean, Old Blue had taught me never to ask for food in case folks didn't have any and they'd be ashamed. So the only way I had of getting what I wanted was just to stare at things until folks asked me if I wanted some.

Old Blue and Charles shook hands and settled in front of the fire to talk. Dory bustled around making coffee and said over her shoulder, "Hambone. That's such a dumb name, Hambone."

"It's what Old Blue gave me," I protested.

"Well, you ought to tell folks your real name," Dory said, clucking her tongue.

"I'll tell my real name when the time comes," I said stubbornly.

Dory smiled and said, "So be it, boy. Now, how about some cake and milk?" I nodded so fast I 'most broke my neck, and I thought I'd never tasted such goodness in my life.

Old Blue and Charles came to the table for their own cake and coffee and when they were settled, Old Blue asked, "Have ye seen Oxalee? Or been bothered by him?"

"No"—Charles shook his head—"I mean, no, he hasn't bothered us. But we have seen him. He usually makes the rounds of all the people at least once during the winter."

"He tried to sell us whiskey," Dory laughed.

"Bought a jug from him, too, for medical purposes," Charles said, "Oxalee does make good whiskey."

"No doubt," Old Blue said dryly and everyone laughed.

"The man ought to be in jail," Dory said. "But so

help me, Blue, I can't keep from liking him." Then, looking sad, Dory said, "From what the radio says, Blue, it sure looks like there's going to be a war."

"It seems the only way to stop Hitler," Old Blue said. "And stop him we will, one way or another. But war seems the most likely way."

"It's the idea of our boys going, Blue, that makes me so sad," Dory said, and Charles and Old Blue both nodded.

Then after a silence, Old Blue said, "Wal, folks, we got a revival to do. Charles, can we count on ye fer the fiddlin'?"

"I reckon you can," Dory laughed. "He has been driving me out of the house practicing all the time."

"I'm always ready to play music," Charles said. "I had better get to work; Dory has been saving a big fat rooster until company comes. So I better get after him."

"Ye wont me to help ye, Charles, to hem him down?" I asked.

"A young pair of legs are welcome to me," Charles said, and I followed him out the door.

The rooster was big, fat, and red and he could run like a wild turkey. Charles and I were both out of breath when I brought the rooster to the ground with a flying tackle. I handed him to Charles and went around the house to set on the porch to rest, looking down the mountainside at the river gurgling and tumbling.

It was a greenish blue color that flowed over rocks and boulders and I thought I would like to live here, then thought I wouldn't when I started thinking about the farm my uncles had taken from me. It set beside a stream, too, that ran fresh and cold year around and there were big maple and oak trees around the house to keep it cool all summer. It was my home—Pa and Ma had built it for me—and I wanted it fierce. I thought of Ma and Pa and what life would have been like with them, and I knew inside myself that they would hate my uncles for taking my farm; I thought of what it would be like having my place back again.

I dreamed about it until the smell of frying chicken pulled me into the house. I thought frying chicken was the best smell in the world, until I got a whiff of the buttermilk biscuits in the oven. There was fresh churned butter in a blue bowl on the table and homemade blackberry jam. There were mashed potatoes with little rivers of yellow butter running down the sides, string beans and pickled beets, and a pan of gravy bubbling on the stove. Seemed to me Dory outdone herself every time we came, and I thought maybe someday if I ever did wed, it would have to be a woman like Dory, I mean a woman who could cook and stuff.

Charles politely asked Old Blue to give the blessings, but instead of bowing their heads, Dory and Charles crossed themselves. I sort of half bowed and half crossed myself. I mean, just in case their religion was right and Old Blue's was wrong. As a matter of fact, I didn't know much about nothing and wasn't real sure I wanted to learn. I mean, I was reasonably happy the way I was.

After the supper dishes were cleared away and darkness fell, Charles built up the fire in the fireplace to take away the evening chill and brought out his fiddle and banjo. Dory played on rare occasions and I got ready to tap my feet. In fact, there was no way I could have held my feet down when "Sally Goodwin" and "Jump Up Pussycat" rolled out of the room and down the mountainside. Old Blue kept his feet tapping, too, and his head bobbed in time to the music. I thought maybe there was no better feeling in the world than music seeping through your body—I mean, after good food, of course.

When the music stopped I begged for more, but Old Blue said I had to go to bed. I didn't mind too much, for the sheets and the pillowcases were soft and clean and there was a feather bed to sink into.

As always, the next morning I hated to leave Dory and Charles, but Old Blue was in a hurry now. Revival time was almost here.

I didn't look forward to our next stop, no music or good food there. To me it just seemed cold bitterness. I thought even the little plank house looked sad as we rode up. Mary Beth met us on the porch, a tall, slender, dark woman with waist-length coarse black hair, black as midnight, and so were her big eyes.

We stopped at the porch when she said, "Ye ain't walcome heer, Blue."

"I know it"—Old Blue nodded quietly—"I know it, Mary Beth. But I came to ask ye to come to revival."

"Maybe, but not as long as Oxalee's thare," she said in a dead voice.

"Iffen ye change yer mind, ye'll be walcome," Old Blue said gently. Mary Beth nodded and went back into the house. Her coldness was no surprise because we had stopped here before.

Old Blue never talked about it, but I had heard other folks. Mary Beth was so unhappy because she was Oxalee's woman, had been for nigh on twenty years. They said she was sad because Oxalee wouldn't marry her, that maybe Mary Beth loved Oxalee better than her own life. I didn't know if it was true; I mean, I couldn't imagine loving somebody more than my own self.

We got on the mules and rode slowly on toward old man Pasmore's, our last stop before we went on to the revival campgrounds. The spring days were warmer, the sky a dazzling blue. Streams leaked and tumbled down the mountainside from the melting snow high above. A body just wanted to sing inside or dance. It was like the air seeped into your blood.

Old Blue killed a rabbit and I cooked it over the camp fire for our lunch. There would be no food at

Mr. Pasmore's place. He hated company of any kind and preachers most of all. Old Pasmore didn't want anyone around but his old hound dogs and chickens, and he said plain out that he didn't believe in God or nothing at all but himself. He made Old Blue feel sad, but the old man just made me mad.

Nine

Mr. Pasmore's house looked like it was two-hundred-years old to me, but Old Blue said it was more like a hundred. It was made of pine logs, yellow with age, and even had a dogtrot between the two rooms. I had read about dogtrots in a history book Old Blue had brought home to me, but I had never seen one before. A dogtrot was just a wide hallway that was open on both ends and had two long rooms built on both sides. Blue said that a long time ago, during the summer, folks would put their tables in dogtrots while they ate because a breeze would flow through. The fence around the house was made of homemade palings that had never seen a drop of paint and was now bleached by the sun to a silver-gray.

Mr. Pasmore was standing in the grassless yard, throwing corn to a bunch of Rhode Island Red chickens and acting like he didn't see us beside the mules at the gate, even though there were three blue-tick hounds trying to leap the fence at us, barking at the top of their lungs. For hound dogs, that's loud.

After a while I felt like kicking the snorting, slobbering dogs in the teeth, but was afraid to. Truth to tell, I felt like kicking the old man, too, but he didn't have any teeth—maybe he never did, I thought, looking at his long nose nigh touching his whiskered chin. He was dressed in dirty overalls and was as skinny as a scarecrow, and, with his old straw hat, he even looked like one.

Finally, the dogs quieted and Old Blue said cheerfully, "Ye got company, Lijah."

"Don't need no company, Blue. Got 'nough company and I know preachers, they wont fried chicken, and ye ain't a-eatin' mine." Then he turned to glare at Old Blue.

"Don't wanna eat yer chickens, Lijah," he said, "Jist wont to ask ye to come to revival."

"Might be thare, Blue, might not. Iffen I do, it shore won't be to heer ye preach. Don't hold with

68

preachers none. Preachers think they know ever'-thin', but they don't not by a long shot." Old Lijah cackled.

I glanced at Old Blue from the corner of my eye and he was grinning all over his face. "Wal, iffen ye let me come in, maybe I can learn somethin' from ye, Lijah."

"Ye ain't trickin' me, Blue. Ye ain't a-comin' in. Never had a preacher stick his feet under my table, never will. Ye eat a man's chicken, steal a man's wife, ye even drink his whiskey iffen nobody was a-lookin'. Only one man's walcome in my home, and that would be Oxalee. He knows how to treat a man and when to leave him alone. Makes damn good whiskey, too. Now, ye jist trot on. Might come to revival, might not. I'm a-thinkin' on it."

"Wal, I'll pray fer ye that ye will make it," Old Blue said, and Lijah turned a face to him that was almost green with rage.

"Don't ye pray fer me, Old Blue Tilley. Don' ye dare pray for me. Ye might pray me somethin' I don't wont. Don' wont no preacher a-prayin' fer me. Ye heer me, Blue?"

"I heer ye," Old Blue said gently and kicked his mule away from the gate.

My veins leaped. We were finally heading for the revival grounds, and for me it seemed the mountains and the valley came alive. There was movement everywhere. Birds sang to the top of their

69

voices, built nests, and dived through the blue hazy air, courting. Chipmunks sat on logs and rotten stumps, chattering and scolding, but looking cheerful and alert at the same time.

The squirrels that were born during the winter came out of holes at the top of trees, looking the new world over. Lizards speared across our path and once we seen a red fox slink into the woods. Pale blue sweet williams grew close to springs and creeks and the dogwood budded. Old Blue said the air was like wine; I didn't know about that, I had never tasted wine, although I had read about it in the Bible.

Old Blue sang "Amazing Grace" at the top of his voice and, not being able to help myself, I sang along with him. The mules even seemed in a good mood, and for Brimstone, that was saying a lot.

It seemed before I knew it, we were at the campground, a flat piece of land on the riverbank with thick woods growing up the upper side of the mountain. Some folks were already there. They came in cars, pickups, and a few in wagons. Camp fires burned in front of tents, kids and dogs played, and women gathered in groups to gossip, and the menfolk kept to themselves, talking of hunting and crops. In the middle of the campground was the brush arbor where Old Blue preached, with rows of logs to sit on and a flattop stump for a pulpit.

People greeted us in loud cheerful voices, calling welcomes and invitations to eat at their camp fires. Granny Hassen was there, but I stayed away from her camp fire and went on over to Mazy-June and Sam's to eat with the other kids. The first day and night of a revival was music, fiddling and banjo playing, dancing and courting by the young, visiting, gossiping, and trading by the older folks who hadn't seen each other for a year.

The next day, long tables were set up for the feasting after Old Blue married all the younguns who wanted to be wed. The sun was warm in the open glen and, being full of beans, salt pork, and fried corn cake cooked on a camp fire, I stirred around to keep from falling asleep.

More and more people came as the sun stood noon high, sitting up their camps and trying to keep kids and hound dogs from going plum crazy. I walked over near a group of women and they were talking about gardens, canning, cooking, and younguns, the first birthing ones, I mean. When one of the women seen me and gave me a dirty look, I walked on like I hadn't heard nothing in the first place.

I didn't stop long at a group of young people, red-faced boys and giggling girls, some holding hands and others making sick-looking calf eyes. It was enough to nigh make me puke. I stayed away from folks my age, too. Girls made me sweat and made my feet and hands feel so big I didn't know where to put them. Boys my age sat up targets and shot their peashooters at them. Baby stuff, I squawked to myself, but sort of wished I had a pea-shooter of my own.

I eased up behind the men to listen for a while. They were squatting on their heels, their hats pulled low, smoking Bull Durham and Prince Albert tobacco. Some were talking trade and others crops and a few were sort of sneaking sips from a jug they passed around, keeping a sharp eye out for Old Blue and their wives.

I looked around for Oxalee and seen his pickup parked clear across the campground near the trees. I knew it was full of whiskey jugs and half-pint fruit jars full of the stuff. I also knew that during the dancing tonight more than a few men and big boys would be there to sample Oxalee's wares and more than a few would be getting dog drunk, like old man Davis.

Sam Horton and Jeb came carrying guns and I thought maybe they would shoot Oxalee because they still thought he was the one who touched Pretty Girl. But I seen Old Blue meet them and talk to them in a low voice and they went to their camp and left the guns. Clem and Pretty Girl were there, too, holding hands for the world to see, and I knew they had come to wed.

Charles and Dory came in an almost new pickup, with a mattress in the back for sleeping and baskets of food, and I made up my mind to stick close to Dory come mealtime.

In the meantime, I decided to go hang around Oxalee's truck to see what was going on. I mean, I was sort of curious to see who was drinking whiskey. I eased through the people. Some sort of patted me on the head and others didn't see me at all. I was surprised to see old Lijah Pasmore at Oxalee's place, but not surprised at all to see old man Davis. Out of the corner of my eye, I seen Miss Rosemary drive in, but I kept on going.

Already some of the menfolks and Charles were tuning up their fiddles, banjos, and guitars. It sounded real cheerful. Oxalee, old Lijah and old man Davis were squatting on their heels, passing the jug and smoking pipes. Jeb and Sam Horton were there, too, and I was startled to see them sip from the jug.

"Wal, boy. Ye come fer a drop?" Oxalee grinned at me, his black eyes dancing and white smile flashing.

Old man Davis snorted, "He's the preacher's whip, won't never be man 'nough to take a slug of whiskey."

I felt my face turn red, and Oxalee laughed, "Now, Davis, don't judge the meanness of a bear by his hide. This youngun might be a grizzly under them freckles."

Old man Davis snickered, "He'll more apt to hide behind the Bible, like Old Blue, 'fraid to be a man."

I felt mad clear to my toes. "I ain't a-hidin' behind nothin'," I snapped, "not a Bible or Old Blue, either."

"Now, boy. Now, boy," Oxalee said. I was so blind with anger, I took the jug.

Ten

I don't know why I did it, but I took the jug to my mouth and gulped drink after drink and didn't realize it was killing me until Oxalee slapped the jug away from my hand. I was on fire and couldn't breathe. I gulped and gasped for breath. Tears run from my eyes and snot from my nose. I held on to the side of the truck, knowing I was dying.

Then suddenly a strange thing happened, a warm glow started at my belly and spread all over my body. I could breathe, the world was beautiful and I loved everybody on earth so much I could cry. I even tried to hug Oxalee, but he laughingly pushed me away, while Sam Horton said harshly, "Old Blue will kill ye, Oxalee. Kill ye deader than a doornail."

"I ain't worried 'bout Blue Tilley," Oxalee said quietly. " 'Tis the boy. He drank a lot of whiskey down."

Old man Davis cackled and Lijah grinned, but Sam Horton and Jeb looked worried. "See, I'm a man!" I mumbled. "I am a man!"

"Shore ye are, boy," Oxalee said. "Now, let's see iffen ye can walk. We best git ye back to yer camp."

I started to move, but the ground rose up and tilted under my feet so high that I had to crawl up it on my hands and knees. I didn't remember where I was going; time had no meaning.

Somehow, Old Blue was there, bellowing like a beat bull, "Oxalee!" I was picked up and carried to the edge of the river and then I was sailing through the air; I landed in the middle of the icy cold water. I came up swimming and gasping, and by the time I got to the bank, I was puking up river water and raw whiskey and it felt like at least five gallons in me.

When I could talk, I turned blazing eyes on Old Blue and said accusingly, "Yer a-tryin' to kill me!"

"I ain't a-tryin' to kill ye, boy. Jist git the whiskey out of ye before it did."

I didn't argue 'cause the world was sort of spinning around me, and I let Old Blue lead me to where our bedrolls lay. He pulled me some dry overalls and a dry shirt out of my bedroll and led me staggering into the woods to change.

I wished the world would stop spinning, it was making me feel sick again. I couldn't think good, but I knew one thing for sure I didn't want as long as I lived was another drink of whiskey. Old Blue led me back to my bedroll and I crawled in, digging my hands into the ground to keep from falling off the earth, and that was the last thing I remembered.

When I woke up, Old Blue was squatting on the ground beside me, gently wiping my wet hair out of my eyes. I felt pale and weak, but my bedroll stayed still. "Ye mad at me, Blue?" I stammered.

"Nope, I ain't mad," Old Blue said, "jist sorry to see ye git drunk."

"Ye don't have to ever worry 'bout me ever a-doin' that ag'in," I said weakly. "Ye shore ain't a-gonna see me a-drinkin' whiskey anymore."

"Wal, thank God fer that," Old Blue said. "Maybe it was a good thin' fer ye to learn young."

"Don't see why folks wont to make themselves sick as a mule," I said, shuddering. "Ye gonna whip on Oxalee? 'Cause, if ye be, ye outta know it wasn't Oxalee who got me to drink. 'Twas old man Davis a-sayin' ye wasn't a man to me. Oxalee didn't know I was a-gonna grab the whiskey jug."

"Maybe so," Old Blue said, "but he was the one

77

who brought it heer, and boy, don't pay old Davis no mind. His head is 'bout eat off with whiskey and he wouldn't know a man iffen he locked horns with one."

"Ye don't hide behind yer Bible do ye, Blue?" I asked.

It was a while before he answered; then he said quietly, "Reckon I al'ays hold the Bible before me. Sort of so folks will know God is thare. But I never held it up to hide behind, and maybe it's time some folks knew it. Now, git some rest, boy. Thare's some weddin's to do and a lot of dancin', too, I reckon, from the sound of the music."

When I opened my eyes again it was dark. Camp fires leaped cheerfully and the smell of cooking food was in the air. I was feeling good again and went in search of Dory and Charles' camp fire. Miss Rosemary and Old Blue ate at Dory's camp fire, too. She fed us venison stew, fried bread all crisp, and there were all the gingerbread cookies I could eat from a big basket. The campground was almost as light as day with all the camp fires and the moonlight.

Charles and some of the other menfolks stood by the stump Old Blue used for a pulpit, playing "Here Comes the Bride" as best they could. Old Blue stood behind the stump, his Bible open. Folks sat on the logs that made two rows and the young people being married marched between them. They came in pairs holding hands, faces blazing red. Clem and

78

Pretty Girl came last because he had to walk so slow.

Some of the womenfolks sort of sniffled and wiped their eyes. All the couples lined up in front of Old Blue and he read the wedding vows; then afterward they murmured, "Yes" and, "I do"; then Old Blue prayed for them, and just after he said, "Amen," Charles's fiddle broke out and started a foot-stomping dance tune; a few seconds later the other players joined him and the fun began.

Everybody was rushing to the flat ground between the brush arbor and Oxalee's truck. Big red-faced overall-clad boys were swinging red-faced laughing girls in dance after dance; even some of the old people jigged a little and some of the younger kids leaped about, clapping hands with the music. Menfolks eased out of the firelight toward Oxalee's truck and came easing back later, looking smug and bright-eyed. Older people watched the young with enjoyment on their faces, and young mothers looked like they wished they were that young again, still courtin', I mean.

The night seemed to spin by on wings. Babies whimpered tiredly, and, just as tired, their mothers put them to bed in tents or pickup beds. Some of the big boys got in fights and Old Blue and other menfolks broke them up. Most of them fought because they had visited Oxalee's truck too many times. More than one man was staggering and it wasn't from tiredness. Daybreak wasn't far off when the men finally got too tired to play any more music and people dragged themselves to their tents. Old Blue and I were the last to go to bed.

I woke with the sun high and the most wonderful smell in the air. Today there would be feasting. No one would eat until evening, then they would stuff themselves. Feast day was sort of like Christmas and Thanksgiving rolled into one.

There were spits turning on the fires, a whole deer on one and a big fat pig on the other. Women were dragging out baskets full of pies, cakes, jams, and jellies and pickles they had saved until this day. Other folks were killing live chickens they had brought and frying them over the camp fires. I felt like if I didn't get something to eat, I wouldn't live until evening, but I knew I would.

Most of the men that gathered around Oxalee's truck were trading dogs or just talking. Old Blue sat in the sun reading his Bible, and every now and then he would peer over at Oxalee's truck. The new married folks took walks in the woods and turned beet red if anyone looked them in the eye.

Mary Beth showed up and stood like a dark shadow under the trees by Oxalee's truck. Old man Davis staggered through the camp trying to talk to folks, but his speech was so slurred no one could understand him. Clem and Pretty Girl held hands and stayed to themselves. Sam Horton and Jeb hung around Oxalee's truck sipping whiskey and talking about war.

I eased all over the camp, looking and listening. Miss Rosemary talked to women about doctoring younguns and stuff like that, and over it all was the smell of the roasting meat. I thought it was a great day, my favorite day of the revival.

Then, with a sad lonesome feeling, I felt that I would miss revivals when I went home again. Truth to tell, I would miss Old Blue, too. I didn't always agree with him and at times wasn't even sure I liked him, but I had a feeling for him of some sort. Maybe a feeling I would have had for my pa if he would have lived. I was sort of mixed up about it. But for right now, it was just a good time to be lazy, I thought, and then decided not to think at all.

The sun was warm, the birds singing, and the sound of voices, old and young, playing. I sat on a log and just let the peace of it soak into me.

Loud voices broke into my dozing and I came wide awake. The voices were coming from Oxalee's truck and I seen Old Blue and a mass of men all trying to talk at the same time. I saw Sam Horton and old Lijah standing toe to toe like they were ready to beat each other to a pulp, but really I knew Sam wouldn't hit a man as old as Lijah.

A lot of womenfolks stood staring toward the truck, but none of them went. I guess they figured it was men's business. I headed for the truck, wanting to know what was going on. I pushed passed old man Davis, looking passed out on his feet, and edged into the middle where Old Blue and Oxalee stood eye to eye. Oxalee looked blazing hot and Old Blue's eyes were cold. I thought it looked like we were going to have a war of our own right here and I felt afraid and whole lot proud that Old Blue was standing up to Oxalee for once, instead of preaching love and mercy at him.

I held my breath as Oxalee spit, "I say yer a coward, Blue Tilley! A coward hides behind a Bible and the skirts of women! Ye wouldn't fight iffen ye got slapped, Blue." Oxalee laughed and a few of the men snickered.

"Maybe not the first time, Oxalee," Old Blue said in a quiet voice. "The Bible says to turn the other cheek, but iffen it's hit, too, I reckon a man would be a fool to stand and git beat to death." There were unbelieving gasps as Oxalee slapped Old Blue on both cheeks quick as lightning, then danced away.

Old Blue's face dropped a little, but he said nothing, just took off his coat and handed it blindly toward me. I took it and backed up, my heart pounding, not knowing this cold man. No kindness or warmness about him now.

"From now on, ye'll not brin' yer whiskey to our revival, Oxalee," Old Blue said as men quickly stepped back, leaving an open space around Old Blue and Oxalee.

"Ye'll not tell me whare to brin' my whiskey, Blue," Oxalee said. " 'Tis my business iffen I wont to sell and men's business iffen they wont to drink it."

" 'Tis my business iffen ye brin' it to revival. I am the preacher heer, the people's leader. 'Tis a branch of the church that sends me on the circuit and to revival. 'Tis a place whare folks meet to share the love of God with each other, not a place fer a drunken orgy, and I'm a-tellin' ye now, Oxalee, I'll have no more of it! Iffen menfolks wont to buy whiskey and drink it, that's none of my business, but heer on church grounds it is."

Pow! Suddenly Oxalee's fist shot out, cracking Blue on the cheek, then like lightning fists were flying everywhere and men ran backward to get out of the way. Flesh met flesh as the two men swung toe to toe and I found myself backed up beside Mary Beth, who was standing quietly, nothing showing on her face as she watched the fight.

The men fought to the riverbank, all of us silently following. Blood flowed from their noses, their eyes were puffed half-shut, but still they fought. Old Blue knocked Oxalee into the water, then went in after him, fists pumping; then they were back on the land, dripping water and still fighting.

"How come they hate each other so bad?" I

asked, feeling sick. "How come Oxalee is a thorn in Old Blue's side?"

I didn't expect an answer, but Mary Beth said softly, "Old Blue ain't exactly been a rose to Oxalee. They were the best of friends some years ago—they were even closer than brothers."

"What happened?" I asked, forgetting the fight for a moment.

"Like twins they were," she went on. "Never seen one without the other. Then a girl moved to the mountains, a girl more beautiful than Pretty Girl. She was small and fair, her hair like spun honey, her cheeks and lips as pink as wild roses. Her eyes were bluer than the sky in April, but she was bad, real bad. Only Old Blue and Oxalee couldn't see it. They were both in love fer the first time in thar lives and they fought bitterly over her. All the time, she was leadin' them on, makin' them both think that each one was her choice. I watched and watched," Mary Beth said, her voice breaking a little; then she said softly, "I can't remember a time I didn't love Oxalee. Anyway, while Old Blue and Oxalee were fightin' over her, she ran off with some other man. Blue Tilley turned to God and the church, Oxalee to the jug and whiskey makin', and a little to me. I wasn't proud," she said bitterly. "I jist wonted to be his woman."

A sort of moan came from the group of men and I ran forward to see Old Blue and Oxalee staggering, acting as if their fists weighed a hundred pounds each.

Someone ought to stop them, I thought, and as if to read my mind, Mary Beth put a hand on my shoulder saying, "No, no. Let them git it out."

"But they are a-killin' each other," I whispered. Both men's faces were like raw meat and their eyes just little slits. Suddenly, I didn't feel like a kid anymore, like in some way I had grown up. The men were murmuring among themselves, saying it was the best and longest fight they had ever seen.

Then so quick it jarred my mind the fight was over, and Old Blue and Oxalee sat on the ground with their arms around each other; their faces were so messed up that it was a while before I realized they were laughing. Then the other men started to laugh, too, and gathered around Old Blue and Oxalee, slapping them on their backs.

I wandered back to our camp carrying Old Blue's coat, feeling sort of lost and more than a little lonesome. Miss Rosemary passed, carrying her doctor bag to go to work on Oxalee and Old Blue.

I thought about home. Maybe I was old enough now to go back and face my uncles and take over the farm that belonged to me. With a war coming on, Old Blue said, raising food would be most important. I could do that, maybe not much at first until I got bigger, or maybe I could get a man too old to go to war to help me. I would miss Old Blue, miss him fierce. But he had Oxalee back now. I longed to hear my name called again. The name my mother gave me. I lay on my bedroll and slept a little, my mind made up: After revival I was going home.

I woke to find Old Blue saying, "Come on, boy. Let's eat." His face had patches of tape and one hand was bandaged; even his lips were swollen together. Through the slits of his eyes, I could tell they had a happy gleam in them.

I could hear the clatter of forks and knives and ran to the river to duck my head to wake up good. The long tables were sawhorses with planks across them that the menfolks had brought in their pickups. Afterward, they would haul them home again. I was so hungry, I didn't know where to start. I heaped my plate high with the crisp, brown pork and thick venison steak. There was fried bread and beans to go with it and all sorts of pickles, but I wasn't in no hurry. I mean, everyone would go back for plate after plate.

Halfway through the meal, Oxalee came up leading Mary Beth and said, "Blue, ye got time fer 'nother weddin'?"

"I al'ays got time," Old Blue said, grinning, and hurried to get his Bible.

All of the folks gathered around while Old Blue wed Oxalee and Mary Beth. Then Miss Rosemary came up and hugged her and so did Dory and some of the other womenfolks. Oxalee brought out a jug and passed it around to the men and I nigh choked when Old Blue grinned and took a sip and said, "I'll sip a little fer yer weddin', Oxalee." Everybody looked surprised, but Old Blue wouldn't take any more than the one sip.

"Won't be none of this at yer preachin' tomorrow, Blue," Oxalee said, and Old Blue nodded, and we all went back to feasting.

The moon was rising as I finished up on chocolate cake and raisin pie. Everybody was full and tired; babies whimpered, some of the little kids bellowed with open mouths, and the women hurried to get them to bed. Everybody went to their camp early. The only sound left was the crackling of the camp fire and the hoot of owls.

Old Blue slept restless and I reckon he must be hurting more than a mite, I slept like a log and it seemed I had just shut my eyes on the moon when the sun picked them open again. Everybody else was up drinking coffee around the fires, feeding kids and rushing because it was revival time and almost time to go home.

Old Blue's eyes were nigh swollen shut and he kept prying them open with his fingers, but they wouldn't stay that way. I rolled up our bedrolls, already to tie on the mules, and brought Old Blue a mug of coffee.

Womenfolks scrubbed kids clean in the river

and put on their best clothes. By midmorning all the folks were lined up on the logs and the brush arbor, even Oxalee and Mary Beth. Old Lijah sat on a log behind Miss Rosemary watching the sun make gold with her hair.

It was dead quiet when Old Blue walked up behind the pulpit and said in a clear, ringing voice, "Friends and neighbors, due to an unforeseen accident, ye might say, I am unable to read the Bible today." He paused, and a few folks laughed out loud.

Then Old Blue held up his hand for quiet, and when it came, he said, "I wont to talk to ye today 'bout us. 'Bout us, friends and neighbors. They's a war a-comin', 'tis plain to see, and I reckon some of us won't be heer next year, maybe never ag'in a'tall and ye young folks a-goin' needs to know God, as well as the folks left behind. God can be a bridge betwixt us no matter whare we go or how far we are. Left to himself, man is a lonely creature. Reckon he al'ays has been ever since he was alienated from God in the Garden of Eden and reckon he'll al'ays be lonesome till he's united with God ag'in. Ye can be united with Him by comin' to this altar and givin' yer life into God's keepin'."

"Amen," some of the menfolks called, and Granny Hassen yelled, "Glory, glory, hallelujah!"

Then Old Blue went on: "Of all the thin's folks need in this world, they need God most, 'cause He's the only one thare when we leave this world fer good, and I don't think we outta wait until the last minute to realize jist what He means to us. It's real simple, folks; when it comes right down to it, God is all and ever'thin' to us. To ye young men a-goin' to war it will seem at times that God is far away. But He can and will go right with ye if ye let Him inside of ye, in yer hearts. Oh, I know some folks say they can't see God, but ye can feel Him. Ye can heer the wind, ye can feel the wind, but ye can't see it, but ye know it's thare. That's the way God is, He's thare."

I felt an ease come over me, like I was listening to Old Blue for the first time. I thought maybe it would be a good thing to have God with me when I went to fight for my home back.

I sort of came to myself to see old Lijah standing up, pointing and saying, "I didn't come heer, Blue Tilley, to heer ye howl. I come to git me a woman and I wont her," he said, pointing at Miss Rosemary.

Old Blue peered from behind the pulpit and said in his deep voice, "Wal, Lijah, ye can't have her. Reckon she's spoke fer, iffen she'll have me."

Miss Rosemary's face lit up like a Christmas tree and even old Lijah knew it was no use. Another easy feeling came over me. I could leave Old Blue now with peace of mind. I mean, he had his best friend back and Miss Rosemary, too. I didn't hear much of the rest of the preaching, I was too busy thinking about being a man in my own home. Maybe, with part of Pa in me and part of Old Blue, I could at least

be a brave one, and Ma had given me a good name:
John Mark Goodman.

I came back to myself with Old Blue shouting,
"Hellfire and brimstone" left and right, and women
shouting and old men yelling, "Amen, Blue. Amen."

The whole arbor seemed to spark and crackle
with excitement and when folks stood up to sing
"Footsteps of Jesus" some were already going to the
mourners' bench to get themselves right with God. A
man ought not to fear finding God for himself, I
thought, and stepped out into the aisle. Later, I will
talk, talk to the man who loved his people.

Hey hi, hey hi ho.
Old Blue Tilley's
a-gonna save some souls.